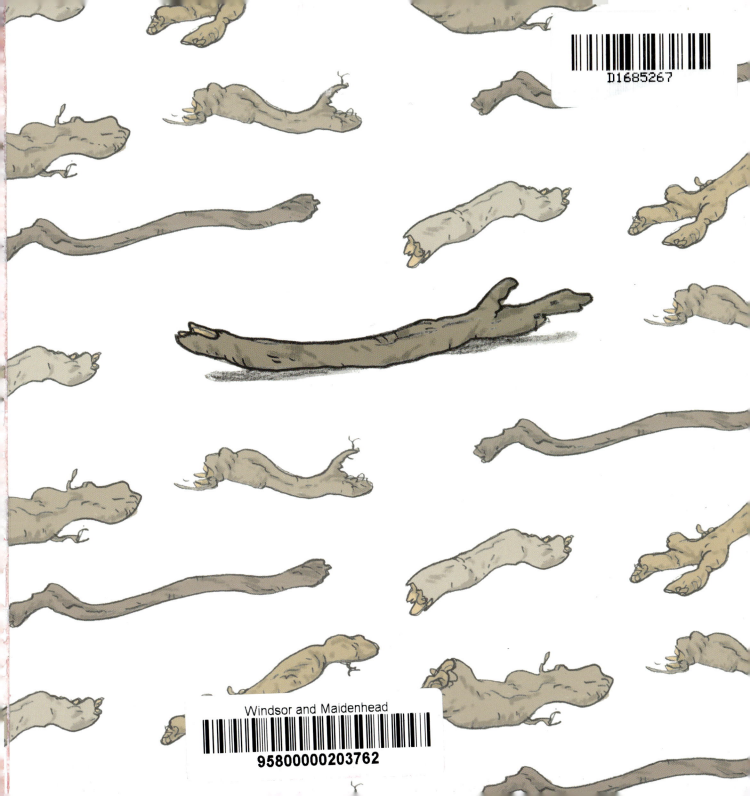

For Shamoddy & Gnoccolinus

WALKIES!

First published in Great Britain in 2022 by
Bog Eyed Books,
39 Coptefield Drive,
Belvedere,
Kent, DA17 5RL

1 3 5 7 9 10 8 6 4 2

Printed and bound by comicprintinguk.com

Logo designed by baxterandbailey.co.uk

British Library Cataloguing in Publication Data:
a catalogue record for this book is available from the British Library

ISBN 978-1-9163118-2-4

bog-eyed-books.com

WALKIES!

by
DAVID ZIGGY GREENE

This is Rosie.

WALKIES!

There is one thing she loves most.

She loves going for walkies.

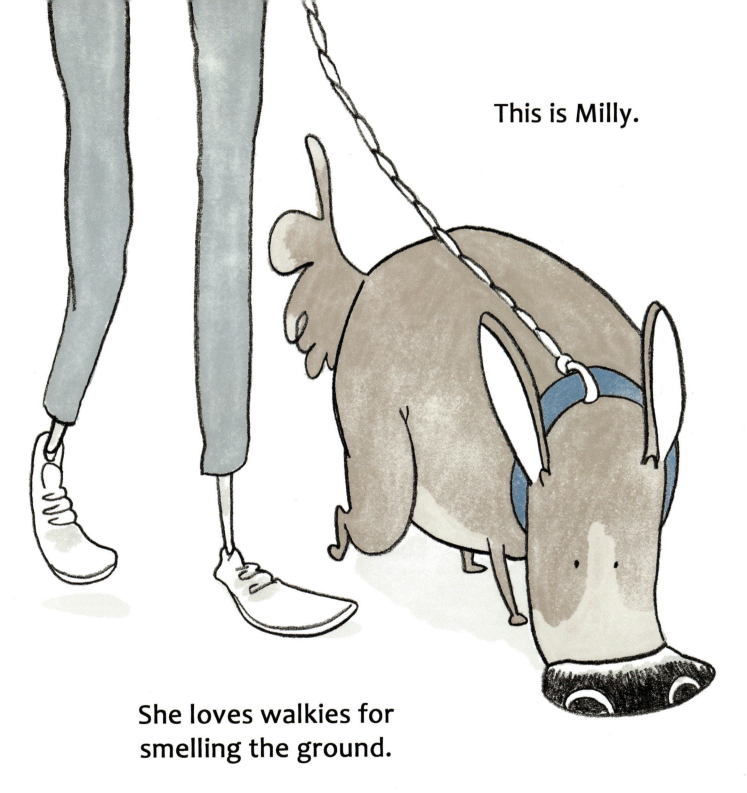

This is Milly.

She loves walkies for
smelling the ground.

To see what dropped food can be found.

MILLY! NO!

This is Norman.

He loves walkies when it's stopped raining,

because that's when the puddles are best!

This is Toddy.

He loves walkies to smell
the bushes and hedges,

because they are the best
places to go to the toilet.

This is Charlie.

He's old but still loves walkies.

At his own pace.

This is Lola.

She loves walkies
with familiar
challenges.

To guide her owner home safely.

This is Pixie and Petal.

They love walkies so much.

That they have to tell everyone about it.

This is Oliver.

He loves walkies in the busiest places.

For all the scratches.

This is Bella.

She loves
walkies on
her lead.

This is Duke.

He loves walkies
to find sticks.

And take the biggest one home.

And when it's
home time,

Rosie loves to
prepare for the
next walkies.

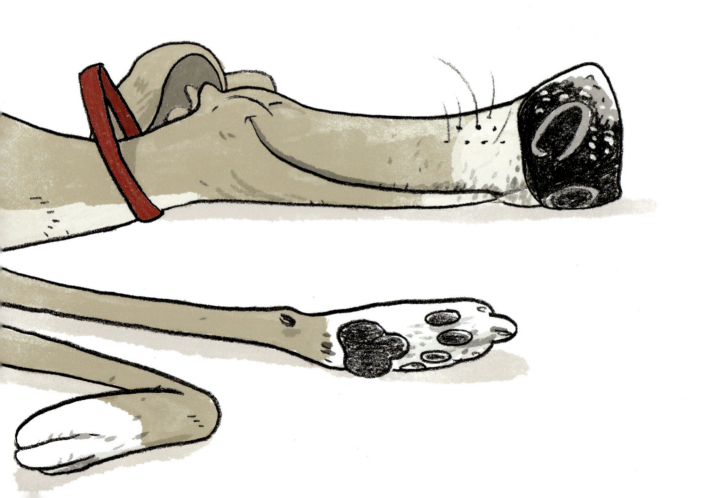

David Ziggy Greene is a house-trained illustrator that draws in the big,
smelly city of London. David's drawn most things as best he can, which
means that he has been published and read by millions around the world
for his illustration journalism and lots of funny comics and cartoons.
He finds dogs great to draw because they are so silly looking in real life,
but they just don't care. WALKIES! is his first ever children's book.
He was inspired by how many people loved his dog drawings.